A NOTE TO PARE[

Reading Aloud with Your Child

Research shows that reading books alo *valuable support parents can provide in helping children learn to read.*

- Be a ham! The more enthusiasm you display, the more your child will enjoy the book.
- Run your finger underneath the words as you read to signal that the print carries the story.
- Leave time for examining the illustrations more closely; encourage your child to find things in the pictures.
- Invite your youngster to join in whenever there's a repeated phrase in the text.
- Link up events in the book with similar events in your child's life.
- If your child asks a question, stop and answer it. The book can be a means to learning more about your child's thoughts.

Listening to Your Child Read Aloud

The support of your attention and praise is absolutely crucial to your child's continuing efforts to learn to read.

- If your child is learning to read and asks for a word, give it immediately so that the meaning of the story is not interrupted. DO NOT ask your child to sound out the word.
- On the other hand, if your child initiates the act of sounding out, don't intervene.
- If your child is reading along and makes what is called a miscue, listen for the sense of the miscue. If the word "road" is substituted for the word "street," for instance, no meaning is lost. Don't stop the reading for a correction.
- If the miscue makes no sense (for example, "horse" for "house"), ask your child to reread the sentence because you're not sure you understand what's just been read.
- Above all else, enjoy your child's growing command of print and make sure you give lots of praise. *You are your child's first teacher — and the most important one. Praise from you is critical for further risk-taking and learning.*

— Priscilla Lynch
Ph.D., New York University
Educational Consultant

To Steve
— G. M.

To Grant Geary
— B. L.

I would like to thank Betsy Molisani and her wonderful first-grade class, Coach Connolly, and Edward Kennedy for letting me go to school with them.

— Grace Maccarone

Library of Congress Cataloging-in-Publication Data

Maccarone, Grace.
    The gym day winner / by Grace Maccarone ; illustrated by Betsy Lewin.
        p.   cm. — (First-grade friends) (Hello reader! Level 1)
    "Cartwheel Books."
    Summary: During gym at school, Sam always comes in last, but a great basketball shot turns him into the hero of the day.
    ISBN 0-590-26263-7
    [1. Basketball — Fiction.   2. Schools — Fiction]   I. Lewin, Betsy, ill.   II. Title.   III. Series.   IV. Series : Maccarone, Grace. First grade friends
PZ7.M127Gy   1996
[E] — dc20   95-10285
                                                                              CIP
                                                                               AC

12 11 10 9 8 7 6 5 4 3 2 1   6 7 8 9/9 0 1/0

Printed in the U.S.A.   23

First Scholastic printing, February 1996

The Gym Day Winner

by Grace Maccarone
Illustrated by Betsy Lewin

Hello Reader! — Level 1

SCHOLASTIC INC.
New York Toronto London Auckland Sydney

It's Thursday.
It is time for gym
for Dan, Jan, Pam,
Sam, Max, and Kim.

Max tags Pam.

Pam tags Dan.

Dan tags Kim.

Kim tags Jan.

But Jan and Kim,
Dan, Max, and Pam —
all of them —
are tagging Sam.

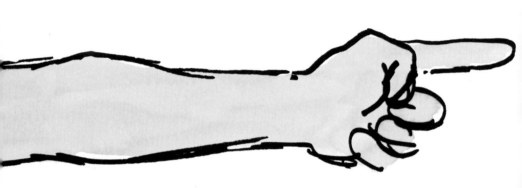

Coach Mike is big
and strong and fun.
He blows his whistle.
He says, "Let's run!"

The children race.
Dan is fast.

Pam is faster.

Sam is last.

Now Jan does cartwheels.
Kim does flips.

Max does rolls.

Sam just trips.

Coach Mike shouts out,
"Go into groups
for three-on-three.
It's time for hoops!"

The children dribble,
pass, and run.

They shoot. They miss.
They're having fun.

Now Dan has two kids
guarding him—
both Pam and Max—

and Jan guards Kim.

But no one guards Sam
because Sam is not fast.
No one guards Sam
because Sam's always last.

Now Dan must pass.
He's in a jam.
Dan throws the ball.

It goes to Sam!

Sam takes a shot.

The ball goes in.
Hooray for Sam!
His team will win.